POPPY

the Pirate Dog

AND THE MISSING TREASURE

POPPY

the Pirate Dog

AND THE MISSING TREASURE

Liz Kessler

illustrated by Mike Phillips

CANDLEWICK PRESS

This book is dedicated to the
original Missy, Miss Havisham.
L. K.

Text copyright © 2014 by Liz Kessler
Illustrations copyright © 2014 by Mike Phillips

First published in Great Britain by Orion Children's Books,
a division of the Orion Publishing Group

First U.S. paperback edition 2016

Library of Congress Catalog Card Number 2013957574
ISBN 978-0-7636-7497-7 (hardcover)
ISBN 978-0-7636-8772-4 (paperback)

15 16 17 18 19 20 TLF 10 9 8 7 6 5 4 3 2 1

Printed in Dongguan, Guangdong, China

This book was typeset in Badger.
The illustrations were done in ink and watercolor.

Candlewick Press
99 Dover Street
Somerville, Massachusetts 02144

visit us at www.candlewick.com

Contents

CHAPTER
One

Poppy the Pirate Dog and her crew
were planning something special.

It was Mom's birthday, so they were going to put on a pirate show to celebrate.

First, they built the ship.

Then Tim and Suzy raised the sails

and George hunted for treasure.

Poppy's job was to guard the treasure and keep it safe.

She was the treasure keeper and
she was a very good one.

Poppy had lots of practice
guarding her bones from George,
so she knew being a treasure keeper
was hard work!

George had just found some
interesting new treasure for Poppy to
guard when they heard Suzy call,
"Ahoy there!"

"Suzy!" It was Mom. "I hope that isn't my best sheet you're using."

"Oops," said Suzy. She lowered the sail and jumped ship. "I'll put it back!"

Then Tim called, "Ahoy there!"

"Do you have my stepladder?" asked Dad.

"Oops," said Tim.

Dad helped Tim take down the ship's front deck.

As Suzy came out of the house, Dad said, "Don't forget, today's Mom's birthday."

"Of course we haven't forgotten," Tim said.

"We're putting on a special pirate show for her!" Suzy added.

"What did you get her?" Tim asked Dad.

Dad smiled. "The prettiest, sparkliest, twinkliest necklace in the world. She's going to love it!"

"Oh, I can't wait to see it tonight!" said Suzy.

Poppy wanted to make sure all the treasure was safe for the show. So she gathered it up and went to look for the best hiding place.

But she had so much treasure in her mouth, she couldn't see where she was going.

Before you could say, "Shiver me timbers!" she crashed into Tim and fell overboard.

Treasure spilled everywhere.

No one noticed that when Poppy
fell, some crinkly paper ripped. And
something shiny and twinkly flew out
and landed on a big round rock.

"Poppy!" Suzy cried. "Are you OK?"

Poppy's eye hurt. Not only had she dropped the treasure, but now she couldn't even see out of both eyes.

I've broken my eye! Poppy thought.

"It looks like she hurt her eye,"
Tim said.

"Poor Poppy," Suzy added, giving
Poppy a squeeze.

The hug was nice, but Poppy's eye
still hurt.

"Come on, Poppy," Tim said. "We need to get you to the vet."

The vet? The man who prodded and poked and sometimes stuck needles in her leg? She wasn't going there! Her eye was fine. It didn't hurt anymore!

She tried to open it. Ouch!

"Wait," Tim said. "I've got an idea."
He ran into the house and came back
with some pirate books.

Poppy lay beside Tim and looked
at the pictures with her good eye.

"Do you see?" Tim said. He was pointing at a pirate surrounded by shiny gold treasure. "That one's the treasure keeper. And look — all the best pirates wear eye patches!"

Poppy studied the picture. Tim was right! She would go to the vet and get an eye patch. Then she would be the best pirate dog again.

CHAPTER
Three

Poppy sulked all the way home from the vet's. She wasn't the best treasure keeper. And she wasn't wearing an eye patch.

She was wearing an enormous, plastic collar around her neck to keep her from rubbing her eye.

Poppy thought it looked like the lampshade in the living room.

She had never felt less like a pirate.

Poppy went straight to her bed. She didn't even get up when the doorbell rang. She just lay there, feeling miserable.

Tim and Suzy opened the door. It was the next-door neighbors Mr. and Mrs. Roy, with their son, Kieran.

"Sorry to bother you," Mrs. Roy said. "We wondered if you'd seen our tortoise, Missy. She was sunning herself outside this morning, but now we can't find her."

Tim and Suzy shook their heads.

"Sorry," Suzy said.

"But we'll keep a lookout," Tim added.

"Thank you," Mr. Roy said.

Before they left, Kieran saw Poppy and burst out laughing.

What are you laughing at? Poppy thought grumpily.

"I thought you said she was a pirate dog," Kieran said. "I didn't know pirates wore giant ice-cream cones on their heads!"

It's a lampshade, actually, thought Poppy as she marched into the yard.

Four

Poppy lay down in the grass. *If Kieran is so mean all the time, it's no wonder that his pet tortoise ran away,* she thought.

Poppy tried to get comfy so she
could nap, but it was hard with the
giant collar around her neck.

As she moved, a ray of sun
bounced off her collar and onto
something in the grass. Something
pretty and sparkly and twinkly.

What was it?

The thing twinkled again.

Was it . . . ? Could it be . . . ?

Pirate treasure!

The treasure was tangled on a big round rock. Who needed a silly eye patch, anyway? This was Poppy's chance to prove she was the best pirate dog after all.

She tugged at the treasure with her teeth. It didn't budge.

Then she jumped in fright.
Because the big round rock suddenly
did something that big round rocks
don't usually do.

It sprouted legs and moved.

Poppy ran into the house and hid under the kitchen table. *Maybe I'm not cut out to be a pirate dog after all,* she thought.

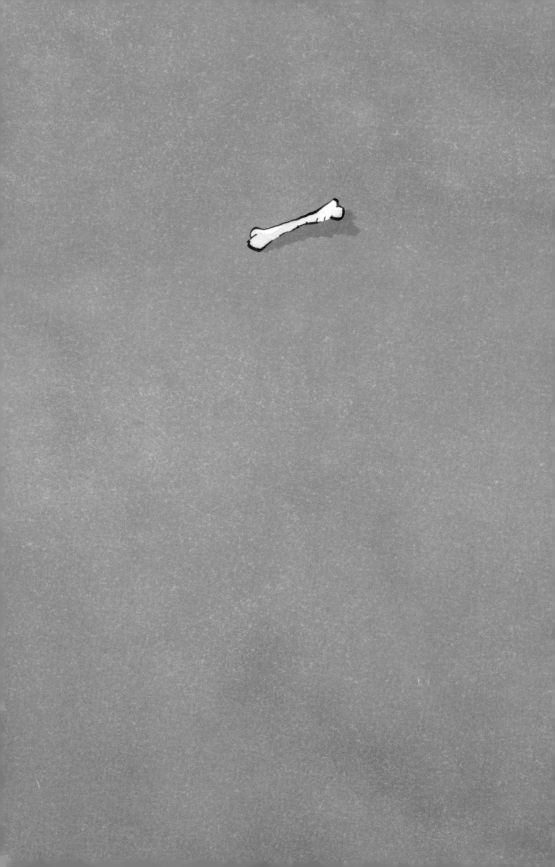

CHAPTER
Five

As she ate dinner, Poppy decided she would try to find the pirate treasure one more time. *I'm Poppy the Pirate Dog,* she thought. *I'm not scared of a walking rock.*

Suzy and Tim were helping Dad clean up in the kitchen.

"When are you going to give Mom her birthday present?" Suzy asked.

"I don't know," Dad said sadly. "I've lost it! I can't believe it. It was so pretty and sparkly."

Poppy's ears pricked up. Pretty?
Sparkly? That sounded like the
treasure she saw outside!

"I wrapped it and hid it under the
bed," Dad said, "but now I can't find
it anywhere!"

Could Poppy's treasure be Mom's present? Poppy ran over and nudged Tim.

Tim gave her a pat. "I can't play now, Poppy," he said.

Poppy ran to Suzy and whined.

"Later, Poppy," Suzy said. "We're busy helping Dad look for Mom's present."

No! Not later! Now! Poppy ran to the back door and whined even louder.

Tim sighed. "Oh, OK. We'll play for five minutes," he said. "Then we've got to find that necklace."

Finally! thought Poppy as Suzy
and Tim followed her into the backyard.
Poppy looked around. Where had
that treasure gone?

Then she spotted it! Poppy moved
her head to make the light bounce off
her plastic collar onto the rock.

The treasure twinkled.

"What's that?" Suzy asked, pointing
at the rock.

"Mom's necklace!" Tim yelled.

"Poppy found it!"

Then the rock stuck out a leg.

Poppy barked.

Suzy squealed.

Tim laughed.

Suzy knelt down and reached carefully for the necklace. "That's not all she's found," she said. She picked up the rock and untangled the treasure from around its legs.

Tim grinned. "She found Missy, too!" he said. "Poppy, you're the best."

"The very best pirate dog in the world," Suzy added.

Poppy wagged her tail. *I am, aren't I?* she thought.

CHAPTER
Six

After they gave Mom her present,
Poppy and her crew got ready to
perform their special pirate birthday
show.

The Roys came to get Missy and
stayed to watch the show.

Kieran even brought Poppy a bone
to say sorry for making fun of her cone.

Tim steered the pirate ship.

Suzy raised the brand-new sails.

George guarded the deck while
Poppy kept a lookout.

And Missy? Well, they had the
perfect job for her.

Missy was in charge of making
sure that none of the treasure went
missing again.

When the show came to an end,
the audience cheered for Poppy and
her shipmates.

Maybe some pirates wear patches on their eyes, Poppy thought when she went to sleep that night. *But only super-special pirates wear lampshades around their necks!*